This story takes place in Australia. All of these animals can be found there.

Text copyright © 1995
by Joy Hulme.
Art copyright © 1995
by Betsy Scheld.
Art direction and book design
by Maria Epes
All rights reserved.
No part of this book may be
reproduced by any mechanical,
photographic, or electronic
process, or in the form of a
phonographic recording, nor may
it be stored in a retrieval system,
transmitted, or otherwise copied
for public or private use, without
written permission from the
publisher.
Scientific American Books for
Young Readers is an imprint of
W. H. Freeman and Company,
41 Madison Avenue, New York,
NY 10010.

Library of Congress Cataloging-
in-Publication Data
Hulme, Joy N.
Counting by kangaroos / by Joy
N. Hulme ; illustrated by Betsy
Scheld.
Summary: When three kanga-
roos come to visit, Sue and Fae
do multiplication to count their
guests' hats, shoes, and the
Australian animals in their
pockets.

ISBN 0-7167-6602-7 (hc)
[1. Multiplication—Fiction.
 2. Arithmetic—Fiction. 3.
Kangaroos—Fiction. 4. Zoo
animals—Fiction. 5. Australia—
Fiction. 6. Stories in rhyme.]
 I. Scheld, Betsy, ill. II. Title.
PZ8.3.H878Co 1995
95-13880
[E]—dc20
CIP
AC

Printed in Hong Kong.
10 9 8 7 6 5 4 3 2 1

KANGAROOS, the largest of the marsupials, are active during the day. They have huge, powerful hind legs and tails. Babies, called joeys, ride in tummy pouches.

SQUIRREL GLIDERS have flaps of thin skin, attached to their wrists and ankles, that stretch out like wings when they take off into the air, allowing them to sail among the trees.

KOALAS do not live in nests or dens. They spend almost all of their time in eucalyptus trees—playing, resting, and eating the leaves.

BANDICOOTS are small, with sharp claws. Their backward-facing pouches protect the babies from being showered with dirt as the mother scrabbles for food or burrows for protection.

WOMBATS dig oversize tunnels with their powerful, sharp-clawed feet. They sleep most of the day curled up inside their burrows and come out at night to eat roots, grasses, and bark.

QUOKKAS are small, chubby, round-eared members of the kangaroo family. They move around on all fours and can climb many feet up into thickets to eat leaves.

NUMBATS feed in the daytime and sleep in the night. Their diet consists of termites, termites, and more termites, which they lick up with quick flicks of their long, tube-shaped tongues.

ECHNIDAS are covered with prickly spines. They have slender beaks, no teeth, and long, sticky tongues to lick up insects—and swallow them whole.

WALLABIES are small kangaroos that come in many different varieties. Some wallabies live in grassy places and can climb trees, while others inhabit rocky areas and caves.

Counting by Kangaroos

A Multiplication Concept Book

Hippity
Hoppity
Boppity
Bee
It's
Time to
Multiply
By
Three.

FOR THE CHILDREN OF EASTERBROOK SCHOOL . . . .

Joy N. Hulme
1997

by Joy N. Hulme

illustrated by

Betsy Scheld

Scientific
American
BOOKS FOR YOUNG READERS

W.H. Freeman and Company / New York

Three hippity, hoppity kangaroos,
With one flat hat and two new shoes,
Came popping along to visit one day.

Sue opened the door and flashed a smile.

Fae said, "Come in and stay a while."

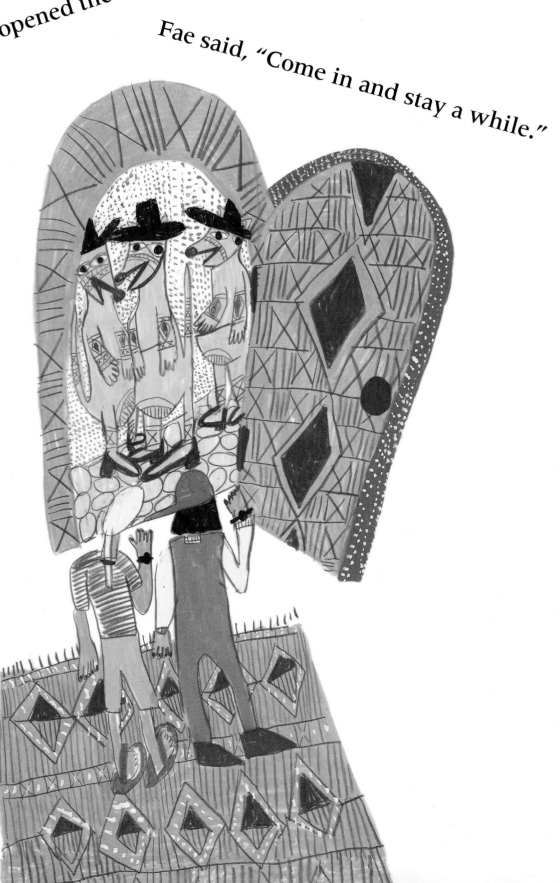

"I'll take your hats,

1,

2,

and 3,

And hang them here

where you can see."

"Slip off your shoes
and rest your feet—

2, 4, 6 slippers lined up neat."

Three kangaroo pockets
were poking out

With lumpity bumps
that squiggled about,

Critters all cramped
and crowded inside,
Australian animals
hitching a ride.

Hippity, hoppity, boppity, bee,

Three crawled out, then three, and three.

Squirrel gliders in a line.
Count them—3, then 6, then 9.

Hippity, hoppity, boppity, bore,

Koalas
came
out
four
by
four.

Soft as cuddly
teddy bears,
4, 8, 12
sat on the stairs.

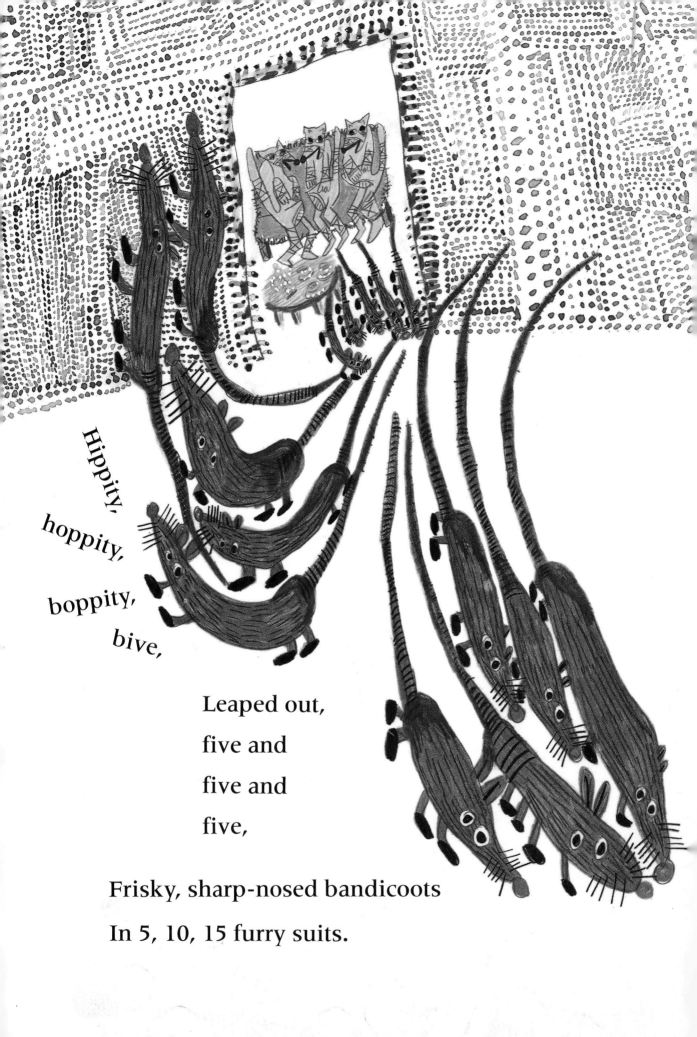

Hippity,

hoppity,

boppity,

bive,

Leaped out,
five and
five and
five,

Frisky, sharp-nosed bandicoots
In 5, 10, 15 furry suits.

Hippity, hoppity, boppity, bix,

Waddling wombats, six by six,

Shuffled slowly down the hall—

6, 12, 18. That is all.

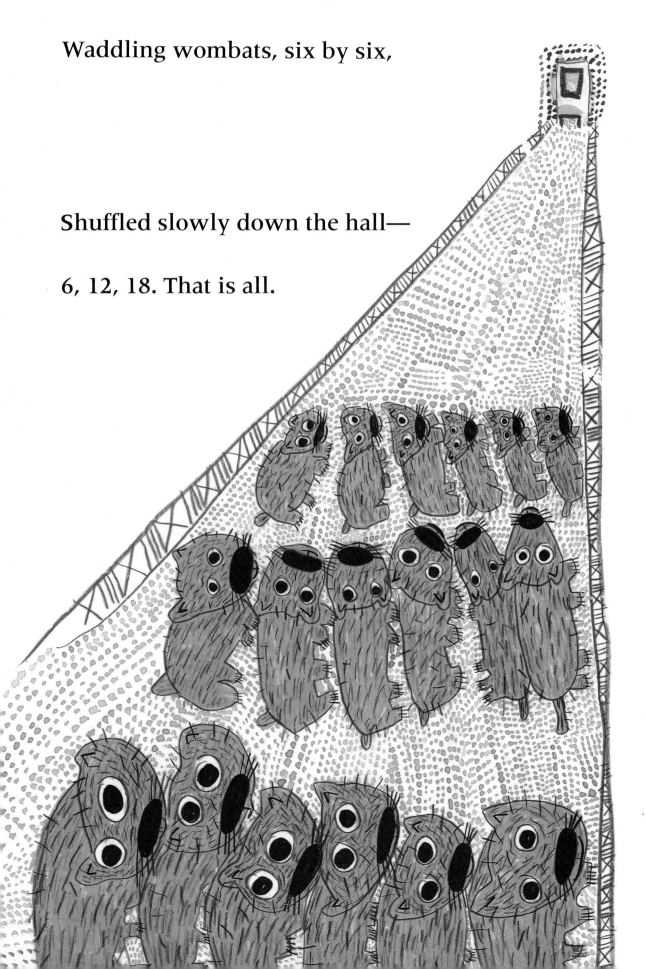

boppity,

Hippity,

hoppity,

beven,

Stocky quokkas,

three times seven,

Bounced on beds
to have some fun—

7, 14, 21.

Hippity, hoppity,

boppity, bate,

Counting out
at eight
by eight,

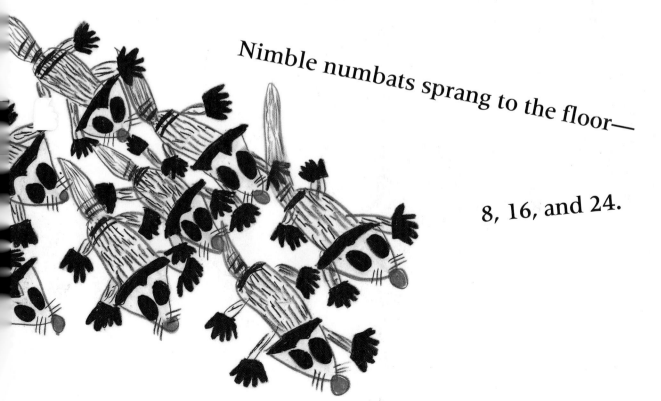

Nimble numbats sprang to the floor—

8, 16, and 24.

Hippity, hoppity,
boppity, bines,

Echidnas, sharp with prickly spines

Came by nines.

It's true, by heaven—

9, 18, and 27.

Hippity, hoppity, boppity, ben,
Bouncing next to count by ten,

Wallaby joeys—

lively, spurty—

10, then 20,
yes, and 30.

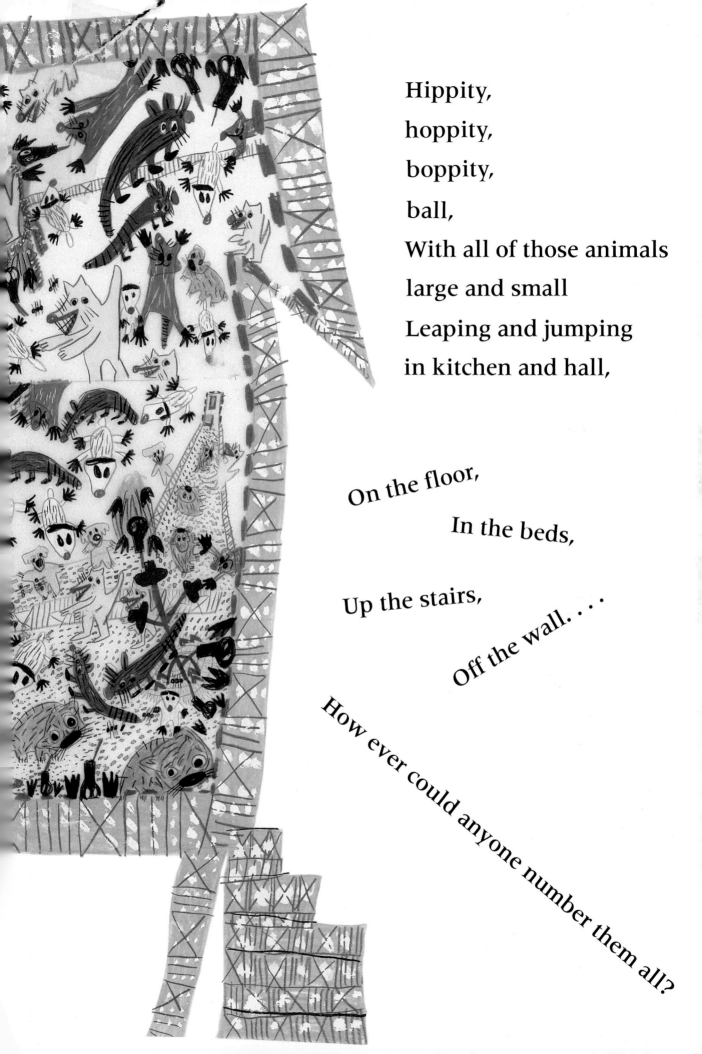

Hippity,
hoppity,
boppity,
ball,
With all of those animals
large and small
Leaping and jumping
in kitchen and hall,

On the floor,

In the beds,

Up the stairs,

Off the wall. . . .

How ever could anyone number them all?

So what did Fae say? What did Sue do?

Fae said, "I give up!"

But Sue. . . .

Sue, she started a zoo.